AGAINST
THE
ODDS

Marjolijn Hof

Translated by
Johanna H. Prins
and Johanna W. Prins

ALLEN&UNWIN

This edition published in 2011
First published as *Een kleine kans* by Marjolijn Hof
Text copyright © 2006 by Marjolijn Hof
Amsterdam, Em Querido's Uitgeverij B.V.
English translation copyright © 2009 by Johanna H. Prins and Johanna W. Prins
Publication of this book has been made possible with the financial support from
the Foundation for the Production and Translation of Dutch Literature
First published in Canada and the USA by Groundwood Books Ltd.

Allen & Unwin
83 Alexander Street Crows Nest NSW 2065 Australia
Phone (61 2) 8425 0100 *Fax* (61 2) 9906 2218
Email info@allenandunwin.com *Web* www.allenandunwin.com

A Cataloguing-in-Publication entry is available from
the National Library of Australia—www.trove.nla.gov.au

ISBN 978 1 74237 508 3

Teachers' notes available from www.allenandunwin.com

Art direction and design by Bruno Herfst
Illustrations (dog, mouse, lettering) by Ann James
Illustrations (watercolour background) by Elise Hurst

Printed in Australia by McPherson's Printing Group

10 9 8 7 6 5 4 3 2 1

For Otto

My father was on his way to a war. His suitcase was packed. He just had to say goodbye.

Every now and then he went off to a war. At least once a year. You're heading the wrong way when you go off to a war. It's better to stay as far away from wars as you can. But my father is a doctor, and they need doctors in a war. My father likes to be needed.

All my father's trips had turned out okay. So far he had always come home in one piece. But I worried that travelling is kind of like jumping rope. For a long time you skip along just fine. But not forever. Sooner or later you miss a beat.

'Don't worry,' said my father.

That didn't help. Travelling is dangerous. Everyone knows that. All kinds of things can happen.

For example, my father could get sick. He could
get malaria. Or yellow fever. And there are tons of
other scary diseases.

'Come on, Kiki,' my father said. 'It's not such
a big deal. I'm super healthy, and I've had lots of
shots.' He pulled up his sleeve to show me where he
had been stuck. I stood on my tiptoes and looked.
There was a small red spot among the freckles on
his upper arm.

'Is that all?' I said.

'And I'm taking pills,' he said.

My father could also be shot dead. There are
tons of soliders in a war. Maybe one of them might
think that my father was the enemy. And then of
course they would shoot him.

'I don't take sides,' my father said. 'Any soldier
can see that right away.'

My father could get into an accident. He could
drive his car into a ravine. Or his plane could crash.

'Do you know the story of the man who was
afraid of everything?' my father said.

'Yes,' I answered.

My father loved telling the story of the man who was afraid of everything. It's a stupid story. The man who was afraid of everything didn't dare leave his home because he was convinced it was dangerous outside. One day a huge tree fell on the house, and the man who was afraid of everything was killed.

'You know what it means,' my father said. 'An accident can happen anywhere. It isn't smart to be afraid of everything and stay home. If everyone stayed home, the world would never change.'

But I would still rather have my father stay home. He could be hit by a stray bullet. Stray bullets are worse than soldiers. They do what they want. They fly through the air and nobody can even see them coming.

'Stray bullets don't exist,' my father said.

'Yes, they do,' I answered.

'Don't worry,' my father said. 'I've never seen one.'

'But when you see one, it's too late,' I answered.

My father leaned over to pet Mona. 'Bye, old girl,' he said. 'Take good care of these women.' He sighed. Mona wagged her knobby tail and sighed back.

'We can take care of ourselves,' my mother said.

My father lifted me up in the air. I put my head on his shoulder.

'You're getting heavy, Kiki,' my father said. 'I can hear my bones creak.'

'Weakling,' I mumbled.

'Sweetheart,' my father answered. He let me down. Then he lifted up my mother. Only a little bit. I listened. No creaking at all.

'The taxi's here,' my mother said.

My father dragged his suitcase to the taxi and

climbed in. My mother ran after him. My father lowered the window and gave her a kiss.

'Kiss!' he called to me.

I climbed up the garden wall and raised my hand. 'Bye,' I said.

The taxi drove away.

Mona can sigh from both ends. Most of her sighs come from her rear end. She lets out soft, stinky little farts. Mona's front end only sighs when you pat her. And I never do.

She was old and dirty when we got her. Nobody wanted her, except for my mother.

Every day Mona gets a little older and uglier. She is small and fat. She has short hair that stands up straight and a little stumpy tail. Her eyes bulge out, she has big ears, and her little teeth stick out from under her upper lip. And from the very beginning she has hated me. If she gets a chance, she lies next to me and farts. One day she bit off half of my name bracelet. Only a little piece was left.

'Now your name is Ki,' my mother said.

'I want a new one,' I said.

'A new dog or a new bracelet?'

'Both.'

'Ki,' my mother said. 'That's not such a bad name.'

My mother loves stuff that's wrecked. Our living room is full of things that normal people would throw out. We have a cracked mirror, a couch with flat cushions and a chair with a broken back. My mother works in a store where they sell secondhand furniture. And when something doesn't sell, she brings it home.

My father doesn't care about stuff. He only cares about people.

My father's taxi drove around the corner. Mona waddled with her short legs down the garden path.

'Too late,' I said. 'He's gone.'

A sigh escaped from Mona's rear end.

We were sitting on the couch with flat cushions. My mother and I. And Mona. Mona was snoring on my mother's lap.

'Do you know about stray bullets?' I asked.

'Don't think about that,' my mother said. I could see from the look on her face that she didn't want to think about stray bullets either.

'But they do exist,' I said.

'I know,' my mother answered. 'But the chances of running into one are very, very small.'

'Maybe Daddy will run into one,' I said. 'Maybe he'll walk into a stray bullet. That's possible. And then I won't have a father anymore.'

'Anything is possible,' my mother said. 'Something can always happen.'

'The story of the man who was afraid of every-thing,' I said.

'That's a stupid story,' my mother said. 'In real life it's much more complicated. I'll try to explain it to you. It's all about something called the odds. For instance, the odds that you'll become a millionaire are very, very small. The odds that you'll find a coin in the street are a lot bigger. You might not know the exact odds of something happening, but you just know there is only a very small chance that you'll become a millionaire. How many millionaires do you know?'

'Not a single one,' I said.

'There you are!' my mother said. 'That's the proof. And it's the same thing with fathers. How many children with a father do you know?'

'A lot,' I said.

'And how many children who don't have a father?'

I had to think for a second. 'Do divorced ones count?'

'No,' my mother said. 'Completely without a father.'

'Just one,' I said. 'John's father died.'

'You see. The odds of having a father are big,' my mother said. 'And the odds of not having a father are small. So you don't have to worry too much about not having a father.'

'Can you make the odds of something smaller?' I asked. 'Or bigger?'

'Yes,' my mother said. 'Sometimes.'

'The man who was afraid of everything made the odds smaller,' I said. 'And Daddy is making the odds bigger.'

My mother sighed.

I knew she was trying to help me. But all this stuff about the odds, about chance, just made everything a lot more complicated. Now I would have to figure out how to make the odds bigger or smaller.

I thought of John's father. The only dead father I knew. I knew three children with a dead cat. And two children with a dead dog. And one child with a dead mouse.

I looked at Mona. I did not know anyone with a dead dog *and* a dead father. A dead dog *and* a dead father! That almost never happened. My mother would say that was against the odds. And it would be even more against the odds for someone to have a dead mouse, a dead dog and a dead father.

'Can I have a mouse?' I asked my mother.

'Why?' she said.

'I want a pet.'

'We have a dog,' my mother said. 'That's a pet.'

I looked at Mona. She was sleeping on the couch. Her tongue stuck out a little from her snout. Now and then she made a smacking noise.

'Mum?' I said.

We went to the pet store. The boy behind the counter gave Mona a dog biscuit. Then he showed me a cage of white mice.

'Why don't you choose one?' my mother said.

All the mice had red eyes and naked tails. They were white and crawled nervously around the cage.

'How old are they?' my mother asked.

'About five weeks,' said the boy.

'And how old can they get?' I asked.

'That depends,' the boy said. 'Two years is average, but sometimes they can get much older. As long as you take good care of them.'

'Which one do you want?' my mother asked.

I pointed at a mouse sitting quietly in a corner.

The boy put his hand in the cage and pushed a couple of mice to the side. 'Look,' he said. 'Just grab him by his tail. Never ever at the tip, but close to his butt.' He pulled the mouse out of the cage.

'Is it a male or a female?' my mother asked.

The boy held the mouse in front of his face. 'A male, I think.'

'And we want a little cage,' my mother said.

'Of course,' said the boy. 'And you might also want to take a bag of sawdust and a night cage. And I'd also suggest a treadmill. And of course a water bottle and a food tray. Perhaps a little toy too.'

My mother was a bit overwhelmed by so many new things. 'A cage and sawdust,' she said. 'And a treadmill. And a water bottle. That's all.'

The boy grabbed a plastic box with holes in the

top. 'A cage like this is the best,' he said. 'It keeps the sawdust nicely in place. But never put it in full sun.'

I nodded.

'And a bag of mouse food,' my mother said.

When we got home I put the plastic cage in my room. On the windowsill. The mouse ran nervously back and forth. He sniffed at the water bottle and the treadmill. I stuck my finger in the cage. The mouse sniffed at it. His nose tickled a bit.

'Squeaky,' I said. Gently, I lifted the mouse by his tail out of the cage. I held him upside down. I saw the bottoms of his paws. They were pink.

I came home from school. My mother was sitting on the couch holding the telephone.

'Is something wrong?' I asked.

'No, no,' my mother said.

'Yes, there is,' I said.

'No, really.'

I sat right next to her. 'Is something wrong with Daddy?'

She gave me a push. 'Don't be silly! What gave you that idea?'

'Well, you know,' I said. 'It's weird the way you are just sitting here.'

'I'm waiting for a phone call from Daddy,' my mother answered.

'I want to talk to him too,' I said.

Mona sat down between us. She let out a stinky sigh.

'How is your mouse doing?' my mother asked.

'His name is Squeaky,' I said.

'Squeaky and Kiki,' said my mother. 'Those names go together very well.'

We sat next to each other on the couch for a little while.

'You don't have to wait,' my mother said. 'I'll call you when Daddy phones.'

My mother knows I hate waiting. Especially waiting together. It seems much more like real waiting than waiting all by yourself. All by yourself you can fake that you are having a good time sitting on the couch. Or you can go and lie down on your bed. You can pat the dog or read a book.

I stood up to go to my room. Mona stretched out full length on the couch, her legs up in the air. She was ready for my mother to pet her.

It was warm in my room. The sun was shining on the windowsill. The inside of the plastic cage was misty. Squeaky sat in a corner. I lifted him up by his tail. I let him loose on my arm. He crawled up to my shoulder. He smelled a bit like mouse pee.

Downstairs the telephone rang.

'Kiki!' my mother called. 'Keeeek!'

I put Squeaky back in the cage and ran down the stairs.

My mother was holding the telephone. 'Yes,' she said. 'Yes, yes...Yes...No...No!...Here too. Really very beautiful. It's almost bikini weather...Not too bad...No, no...Really not...Great...Tuesday? ...It's okay...Here she comes...Bye...Bye, sweetheart...Yes...Bye...Bye...Bye-bye.'

She handed me the phone. 'Dad?' I said.

'Hello Keeks,' my father said. 'I hear it's beautiful weather.' His voice sounded very close. Closer than in real life.

'It's hot,' I said.

'Here too,' my father said. 'But this morning we had fog.'

'And how is it now?'

'Not anymore,' said my father. 'Kiki?'

'Yes?'

'I miss you.'

'Yes,' I said.

'I'll phone again on Tuesday.'

'I miss you too,' I said. 'And I have a mouse.'

'A real mouse?'

'Come on!' I said. 'Of course it's a real mouse.'

'Fantastic!' answered my father. 'Hey Kiki, I have to go now. Bye!'

'Bye,' I said. 'Will you take good care of yourself?'

'Yes,' my father said. 'And you?'

'Me too,' I said. 'And you?'

'Me too,' my father said. 'And you?'

'Me too,' I said. 'And you?'

'Me too,' my father said. 'But now I really have to go. Kiss!'

'Kiss,' I said.

I heard a click and after that a long sound. 'He's gone,' I said to my mother.

She nodded. 'Come and sit for a minute. Would you like a cup of tea?'

'In a second,' I said. 'First I have to go upstairs.'

'Can't you do that later?'

'No,' I said. 'Squeaky's cage is in the sun.'

'Don't let that happen!' my mother said.

'I know,' I said. And I ran upstairs.

For a while I didn't think about my father. I made a night cage for Squeaky from an old pencil box. And I read a book about the police because I had to do a report at school. When I finished the book I was sure I didn't want to be a policeman. That's what I said when it was my turn to speak in class. I said I did not feel like dealing with problems all day long. I would prefer to become a hairdresser or a pilot. Miss Anneke gave me the highest grade because I had given my own opinion.

When I came home my mother was sawing in the middle of the living room.

'I got the highest grade,' I said.

'Wonderful,' my mother said. Her knee was propped on a dresser. The dresser was on its side and had only two legs left. 'For you,' my mother said. 'For your bedside.' She knocked on the top part of the dresser. 'This is where Squeaky's cage can go.' She lifted her knee and opened a little door. 'And this is for food. Or a book. Or something else.'

'Why are you sawing off the legs?' I asked.

'They were wobbly.'

I wanted to say I didn't like old stuff. But it

wasn't too bad, not really. Without legs it was a dresser that would come in handy. 'Okay,' I said.

My mother continued sawing. I picked up the telephone to call Margie. Margie had been my friend for a very long time. But I didn't see her that often anymore. She took violin lessons and gymnastics and she was almost never home.

'Daddy might call at any moment,' my mother said. 'Can you keep it short?'

I put the phone down again. 'Forget it,' I said. 'Margie doesn't have time anyway. She has to practise her somersaults.'

My mother sawed off the last leg. She carried the dresser upstairs and put it next to my bed. And then she started vacuuming.

My father did not call. Everywhere my mother went she took the telephone with her. To the kitchen when she started cooking, and to the yard when we were going to eat outside. Later in the evening she took it upstairs with her. She put dirty towels in the washing machine, she told me to brush my teeth, and she fluffed up my bedcovers. The telephone did not ring.

'You have to wake me up if Daddy calls,' I said.

'No, no,' my mother answered. 'You just go to sleep. Perhaps he'll call very late or not at all. Or maybe tomorrow.'

'I can't sleep,' I said.

My mother closed the curtains. 'It smells like mice in here,' she said.

'I'm not going to sleep,' I said.

My mother took the telephone downstairs with her, and I lay there trying to listen. There were all kinds of sounds – footsteps, the television, the closet door and one time a little bark from Mona.

Squeaky rummaged around in his cage. I could hear him gnawing on something. Then he ran on the treadmill for a while. I had put the cage on top of the dresser. Squeaky made such a racket next to my head that I couldn't hear what was happening downstairs.

The next morning my mother said that my father hadn't called. The next day he didn't phone either. The phone rang often, but most of the time it was my grandmother asking whether we had any news from my father.

'What's happening?' I asked.

'Nothing,' my mother said. 'It's just that Daddy is somewhere in the middle of the jungle and perhaps can't find a way to get in touch with us. It's happened before.'

'You can make phone calls anywhere,' I said. 'Even in the jungle.'

'That's not true,' said my mother. 'Here you can, but where Daddy is, you can't.'

'But where is he?'

'Some place where he can't make a phone call,' my mother said.

'Where?' I asked.

'He's travelling. He's travelling and can't make a call.'

'But I want him to call!'

'Now listen to me carefully,' my mother said. 'Daddy will, soon. He's gone to visit a small hospital, somewhere far away from the city. He's still on his way, I'm sure. Everything is fine.'

'You don't know where Daddy is,' I said.

'I don't know exactly where Daddy is.'

My mother took a map out of the closet and unfolded it on the table. She pointed to a river that twisted and turned through a green section of the map. Her finger followed the river to a light blue spot. 'Here,' she said. 'He's somewhere near this lake. I do know more or less where Daddy is.'

'But you don't know for sure,' I said.

'No,' my mother said. 'Not exactly, because he is travelling.'

The next day my father didn't call either. My grandmother called five times. And so did lots of other
people I didn't know.

I took Squeaky out of his cage a lot. He was
getting tamer. He climbed up my arm and sniffed
my ear. I put him on my head so he could nibble my
hair. Squeaky was alive. You could easily see that
he wasn't about to die. Maybe I should have left
his cage on the windowsill. Maybe he would have
melted. Melted to death in the sun. Then I would
be someone with a dead mouse by now. And the
odds of having a dead mouse and a dead father
were really small.

I thought of five ways to kill a mouse.

1   melting it to death
2   chopping off its head
3   drowning it
4   dropping it out the window
5   giving it to a cat

But when I thought about even one of these ways, I felt sick to my stomach. Now that I knew Squeaky, with his soft hair and his little paws with little pink cushions, I had started to love him. And my father knew about him too.

So I went back to the pet store.

'I want another mouse,' I said.

The boy from the pet store showed me the mouse cage. There were about ten little mice.

'Don't you have any old mice?' I asked.

'Nobody wants an old mouse,' the boy said.

'But I do. I want an old mouse. Or a sick mouse.'

'We don't sell sick mice,' the boy said. 'What is it you really want?'

'I'd really like a very old mouse,' I said.

The boy looked at me. 'Forget it! What for? Do you have a snake?'

'No,' I said.

'But that's normal,' the boy said. 'Some snakes eat mice.'

'It's for school,' I lied. 'At school we're talking about helping others. About old people and sick people and how you have to take care of them.'

'And?' the boy said.

'And old animals,' I answered. 'The ones nobody wants to own anymore, because they'll die soon. First I wanted an old cat from the shelter, but my mother wouldn't get me one. But she'll let me have an old mouse.'

'Okay, then,' said the boy.

I didn't know I was such a good liar. Of course I had lied before, but usually it didn't work. My mother could almost always tell by my face, and at school they hardly ever believed me. But the boy at the pet store looked at me and didn't guess a thing.

'I can get good grades with it,' I said.

'I don't know,' the boy said. 'I don't have any old mice anyway.'

'Too bad,' I said.

For a moment the boy thought it over. 'But I do have a misfit. He'll never make it.' He walked over to a door at the back of the store. 'One minute. Don't touch anything.' He disappeared behind the door. A little later he returned with a small cardboard box. A tiny pink mouse lay in the bottom. It was almost hairless.

'You're not going to mess around with it, are you?' said the boy.

'No, no,' I said.

'And don't put it together with the other mouse.' The boy gave me the box. 'It's a young one, but he's not going to make it.'

The little mouse moved a tiny paw.

'Is he in pain?' I asked.

'No,' said the boy. 'Otherwise I would have done something about it.'

'I'll take good care of him,' I said.

'That's good,' said the boy. 'But he won't last much longer. You know that, don't you?'

I nodded.

A loud voice woke me up. It was my mother. She was standing in the bathroom, holding the phone.

'No,' she yelled. 'You shouldn't call all the time... No... Darn it. It's only six-thirty!... No!... I'll call you... Of course not... Bye!'

'Was that Oma?' I asked.

'Yes,' my mother said. 'That was Oma.'

'Were you having a fight?'

'No. Well, yes we were. She won't stop calling. And every time I think it's Daddy.'

'Then Daddy hasn't called yet,' I said.

'No,' my mother said. 'Daddy hasn't called.'

'Is he going to phone today?'

'Kiki,' my mother said. 'Please!'

* * *

I went to my room to look at the new mouse. He was lying very quietly in his box. He didn't look very alive. But I wasn't sure if he was dead. When I was done getting dressed he was lying there, just the same. And when it was time to go down for breakfast, I still couldn't see any change.

I went to school. It was a little bit strange. Maybe I should have felt sad. A little bit sad, because the mouse was such a tiny little animal and I had just got him.

After school Margie wanted to go home with me. Her violin teacher was sick. Margie had a free afternoon.

'You can come,' I said, 'if you aren't scared of mice.'

'You have mice?' Margie asked.

'I have two,' I said. 'But I think that one of them is going to die.'

'I've never seen a dead mouse,' Margie said.

'Me either,' I said.

'When he is dead, are you going to bury him?'

I hadn't thought about that.

At home I showed Margie the mouse.

'Is he dead now?' she asked.

'I think so.'

Margie put a finger in the little box. 'He's cold.'

I picked up the mouse. Then I knew for sure that he was dead. He was no longer a mouse, I could tell. In my hand lay a little cold thing.

'It's a strange-looking mouse,' Margie said.

'He was a misfit mouse,' I said.

We packed up the box – first a layer of cotton, then the mouse and then another layer of cotton. We took it out to the garden. Margie dug a hole close to a bush. And I put the box in the bottom. Then together we filled up the hole.

———

'Are you sad now?' Margie asked.

'Not very,' I said.

'But it was a little bit scary.'

'Yes,' I said.

I did not dare tell Margie I felt happy. Happy, because now I was a girl with a dead mouse. There were plenty of girls with dead mice. But there were only a very few girls with a dead mouse *and* a dead father. I had made the odds a little bit smaller.

'Were you digging in the yard?' my mother asked.

She didn't know about the mouse. She didn't even know that I had brought him home with me. And she didn't know that he was lying under the ground in a little box.

'No,' I said.

'That's strange,' my mother said. 'Somebody has been digging in the yard. Next to the butterfly bush.'

'Mona,' I said. 'Mona did it.'

'I'll be darned!' my mother said. 'Mona!'

Mona came tottering over, wagging her stumpy tail.

'Bad dog,' my mother said. But she said it in her lovey-dovey dog voice, all high and fakey, and she stroked Mona's head. Mona was crazy about that lovey-dovey dog voice. She tried to wag even harder. She started to sigh from both ends at the same time.

My mother had brought home a bag of French fries. 'Why don't you get a few tomatoes out of the fridge?' she asked me. 'And the mayonnaise.'

We ate the French fries in the backyard, in the shade. We dipped fries and pieces of tomato into the mayonnaise.

'I'm going to change the living room around,' said my mother. 'I have a beautiful buffet at the store. I don't understand why nobody wants it.'

'What's a buffet?' I asked.

'A large chest. With drawers and shelves and little doors.'

'But the living room is already full!'

'First we have to make room,' my mother said. 'The old bookcase has to go. And that's where we'll put the buffet. I still have some work to do on it. I think I'm going to paint it yellow.'

'Yellow?' I said. 'No, no, not yellow.'

'A light shade of yellow, then,' my mother said.

I swirled a French fry in a small puddle of tomato juice on the table.

My mother chattered on about the buffet and about the rest of the living room. 'Everything will be different!' she said.

She was acting very cheerful. More cheerful than she needed to. Sometimes I'm weirdly cheerful when I'm nervous. But my mother isn't usually that way. I'd never seen her so excited before.

'Did Daddy call, maybe?' I asked.

She became quiet right away.

'Yes?' I said.

'No,' she answered. 'No, Daddy hasn't called.' She sighed. 'Kiki, I actually do need to tell you something. Or maybe not. I mean I don't know whether I should or not. I don't know what's best.'

I felt sick. I had eaten too many French fries, and now I felt like my stomach was full of cold dead mice.

'Daddy is missing,' my mother said.

'I don't believe it,' I said.

'Well, it's true,' my mother said. 'Daddy is missing. That means nobody knows where he is right now. But it doesn't yet mean that something serious has happened.'

'Are you scared?' I asked. And I hoped my mother would say no. She had to say no.

But my mother said, 'Yes.' And then she added, 'A little bit.'

She wasn't supposed to be scared. I was the one who was supposed to be scared, and she was supposed to say it wasn't so serious and that I shouldn't exaggerate.

'Come and sit next to me for a minute,' my mother said.

I shook my head. I put my elbows on the table and held my hands in front of my mouth. I bit myself, right below my thumb. Until it hurt.

'At first I didn't want to tell you,' my mother said. 'But you would have heard it from someone else.'

I stopped biting. 'From Oma,' I said.

My mother smiled a faint smile. 'For sure. From Oma. From that busy chatterbox.'

'Does she know already?'

'Yes,' my mother said. 'Kiki?'

I put my hands on the table. There were teeth marks below my thumb. You could see that I had one crooked tooth in the middle.

'It's going to be all right,' my mother said. 'They are going to look for him. It may turn out that nothing is wrong.'

'Are you really going to change the living room?'
I asked. 'Are we really going to have that weird old
buffet?'

My mother shrugged. 'I don't know,' she said.

I dreamed about stray bullets. There were quite a few. They travelled like a swarm of bees through the air. Every bullet had little eyes, a beak and a nose with a sharp point. They looked a little like sharks, but only from the front. They whistled. Not with their beaks. They just whistled. Very high. And loud. It hurt my ears. It woke me up.

It was dark. Squeaky was chewing on a corner of his night cage. That was the only sound. I climbed out of bed and walked into the other bedroom. My mother was snoring softly. I crawled under the covers with her and lay on the spot where my father ought to be.

'Mum?' I said.

My mother woke up. 'What's the matter?' she mumbled.

'I had a dream,' I said.

'What about?'

'About stray bullets.'

My mother sat up in bed and switched on the bedside lamp. 'Oh, my girl!' she said.

'I don't want to sleep anymore,' I said.

'Was it scary?'

'It just started,' I said. 'But maybe it will come back.'

My mother yawned. 'Better not to go back to sleep. Not right away. Do you want tea?'

I leaned against her. I didn't want tea.

'Or a story?'

'Of course not,' I said.

'No, of course not,' my mother said. 'You think it's babyish.'

'I want Daddy to come home.'

'Me too,' my mother said.

For a while we didn't say anything. We leaned against each other without speaking. My eyes almost closed. Right on the edge of my sleep, a swarm of

stray bullets was flying around. I quickly opened my
eyes as wide as possible.

'Mum? Aren't you ever angry with Daddy?'

'Why?'

'When he leaves?'

My mother thought about it for a while. Then
she said, 'No. It isn't always okay with me when he
leaves. But when I met Daddy, he warned me. He
said I should look for another man. A homebody.
But I didn't want another man. I wanted Daddy.'
She grinned. 'And Daddy wanted me.'

'Why isn't Daddy a homebody?'

'You know why,' my mother said.

I didn't answer. Of course I knew why. But it
was nice to hear something I knew already.

'He wants to go out into the world,' my mother
said. 'He wants to help. He thinks there are enough
doctors here. He knows that in other countries there
are too few doctors. Countries with earthquakes or
floods.'

'Or war,' I said.

'That too,' my mother said. 'War.'

'But what about us?'

'When you were born Daddy promised he would

stay home. He really tried. He worked in a hospital. But…'

'But what?' I said.

'But there were too many wars,' my mother said. 'I knew that Daddy really wanted to go.'

'To help.'

'Yes,' my mother said. 'To help.'

'And so you said he could go on trips again.'

My mother said, 'Well…'

'Well?' I repeated. I didn't quite know what we meant by that 'well'. I could barely hold my eyes open anymore.

'Then we made an agreement,' my mother said. 'Daddy would go on trips again, but not as often. And not as long. Because he wanted to be with us too. He wanted both – being on trips and being with us.'

'Did you ever want to go with Daddy?' I asked.

'Oh no,' my mother said. 'Oh gosh, no. I wouldn't want that.'

We leaned quietly against each other. Outside a bird started to sing. Once in a while I slept a little, but then I quickly opened my eyes wide again.

'What are we going to do now?' I asked.

'We can't do very much, Keeks,' my mother said.

More and more birds began to sing. I thought I could close my eyes for just a second. Without falling asleep. But when I opened them again it was a lot later. It was already daylight outside. My mother lay next to me, asleep.

The pet store opened at nine o'clock. By five to nine I was standing at the door. It was Saturday and I didn't have to go to school. The boy in the pet store opened the door for me. I walked over to the counter and stood still.

'And?' the boy said.

'The mouse is dead,' I said.

'We knew that would happen,' the boy said. 'Did you take good care of him?'

'Yes,' I said. 'It was a beautiful death.'

The boy smiled. 'A beautiful death, was it?'

That 'beautiful death' I had picked up from my oma. Once she mentioned that someone nearly one hundred years old had died in his sleep. She called it a beautiful death and a peaceful end.

'And a peaceful end,' I said to the boy.

'I'm happy about that,' the boy said. 'Can I help you with anything? Did you come for mouse food? Or something else?'

'I came for a little dog,' I said.

The boy shook his head. 'No,' he said. 'We don't sell little dogs.'

'It doesn't have to be a young dog,' I said. 'I'm really looking for an old dog.'

I looked at the door at the back of the store.

'A misfit dog would be okay too.'

Perhaps the boy had a lot of misfits behind the door. Of course misfit creatures weren't allowed in the store.

The boy looked at me. 'What are you up to?'

'It's for school,' I said.

'Again? What school do you go to?'

I didn't quite know what to say. If I told him the name of my school, he might call and ask questions. And if I said the name of a different school, he might ask there too. And I couldn't explain to him that I wanted to be a girl with a dead dog. Now I was a girl with a dead mouse. But it would be so much better to be a girl with a dead mouse *and* a dead dog.

'But aren't there any misfit dogs?' I asked. 'Dogs nobody wants?'

The boy leaned forward over the counter. 'Which school?' he asked. 'You haven't answered me.'

'It's not for school,' I said. 'It's for my father.'

The boy looked at me angrily. 'Are you crazy or something?'

'Really. It's for my father,' I said. 'But I can't explain it very well.'

Slowly the boy shook his head. 'This is weird. I can't believe this. Do you think I'm stupid?'

'No,' I said softly.

'Well, what then?' the boy said.

I walked out of the store.

'You have to tell me everything,' I said to my mother.

'I will tell you everything,' she said. 'Well, almost everything.'

We were sitting at the table playing Monopoly. My mother already had three streets with houses. I had all the railroads. 'You're only telling me a little bit,' I said.

My mother threw the dice. 'Nine,' she said. 'Was I using the little hat or the little car?'

'The little hat,' I said.

She moved the hat nine places.

'Mum!' I said.

She looked at me. 'I do hear you, Kiki, but I have to think for a second.'

'About what?'

'About what I should and shouldn't tell you.'

'I want you to tell me everything.'

'But I don't know all that much. In fact I know almost as little as you do. And I'm telling you all the important things. And I can't keep telling you things all the time.'

'Why not?'

'Because it's not good. Because first I hear this and then that. It's all very confusing.'

'But I want to know everything,' I said.

'Maybe that's not such a good idea,' my mother said. 'Maybe it's just like the movies. Some movies are only for eighteen year olds and you're not allowed in. That's to protect you. Maybe I need to protect you a little bit too and only tell you news when I'm sure of it.'

'Margie's brother rented a DVD,' I said. 'It was for eighteen year olds and up, but I saw it anyway and I could handle it quite well.'

'Which movie?' my mother asked.

'*Terror from Outer Space*,' I said.

My mother put the dice in front of me. 'Never heard of it.'

I threw the dice in the middle of the board.

_____

'Eight.' I moved the little car ahead and said, 'It was about aliens. They were sort of space monsters in disguise. They looked exactly like human beings. But they could suddenly appear. They burst open and a monster would come out and gobble people up. Not monster people, real people. You get it?'

'No,' my mother said. 'Not really. But it sounds pretty scary to me.'

'It wasn't at all scary,' I said. 'I didn't mind it at all. Ask Margie. Her brother kept telling us that it was fake. He said everything was made of rubber and it was ketchup instead of blood and then I wasn't scared anymore.'

'But that's different,' my mother said. 'What's happening with Daddy is real. It's giving you bad dreams.'

'That's because I don't know anything,' I said. 'It's because I don't know anything that I get bad dreams.'

My mother picked up the dice and threw. 'I'll try,' she said. 'I'll try to tell you how things are going, but I don't promise that I'll always tell you every-thing. It's just not possible.'

'Okay,' I said.

'I threw twelve,' my mother said.

'You didn't pay attention,' I said. 'I was parked on your street, but now I don't have to pay anymore.'

My mother put the map on the table. 'I'll show you,' she said. She pointed at the river and at the light blue spot. 'Daddy was on his way to a small hospital. It's about here, near this lake. He left in a car. But he hasn't arrived yet.'

'Was he all by himself?' I asked.

'No. I believe there were three cars. But I'm not sure.' My mother drew a square on the map with a magic marker. 'This is where they are going to look for him. This is about where he should be.'

'Why don't we search?' I asked.

'We can't.'

'Why not?'

My mother pointed at a large green section on

the map. 'All of this is wilderness,' she said.

I looked at the map. Some areas were light green. Other areas were dark green. Here and there you could see a small brown speck.

'You need special people for this,' my mother said. 'People who know the forest.' She folded up the map. 'We need to be patient.'

'Are there soldiers?' I asked.

'Maybe. But you need to understand one thing – Daddy is there to help. He has nothing to do with soldiers.'

The map was lying on the table. My mother stared at it. Maybe she was thinking about a forest full of soldiers, just like me.

'How old is Mona?' I asked.

My mother looked surprised. 'Mona? Mona is fourteen. What made you think of that?'

'How old can dogs get?' I asked.

'Not so very old,' my mother said. 'Mona is a very old oma.'

'Oh.'

'You're not starting to worry about her, I hope?' my mother said.

'Oh no,' I said.

* * *

That afternoon my mother went grocery shopping. I stayed home. I was sitting on the couch. Mona was lying close to the armrest with her eyes closed.

'Drop dead,' I said to her.

Mona moved one ear. Nothing else.

'Drop dead,' I said again.

She did not even stir an ear this time. But I knew that Mona was not dead because she always only did exactly what she felt like doing.

That's when I thought of five ways to kill a dog.

1 locking it up without food
2 drowning it
3 dropping it out the window
4 chopping off its head
5 letting an attack dog tear it to pieces

I told myself that Mona was a misfit dog. As much of a misfit as the mouse that I had buried in the yard. And it wouldn't be so serious if she died.

But killing Mona was worse than killing a mouse. I imagined it would take a lot of blood and struggle to chop off Mona's head. I started to feel awfully sick to my stomach. I knew I would never be able to do it. I was not a dog murderer.

'Biscuit?' I said.

Mona opened her eyes. She jumped off the couch and walked over to the cupboard, wheezing. She knew exactly where the bag of dog biscuits was kept.

While I was following her, I thought of a sixth way to kill Mona. I tore open the bag of biscuits and put it on the floor. Immediately Mona put her head in the bag. I heard her chewing and smacking.

'Boo!' I screamed.

Mona jumped back. She started running around in circles and barking like mad.

Margie once told me that it was dangerous to give old people a sudden scare. They might have a heart attack. But it didn't work with old dogs. Mona got a great scare, but her heart didn't stop. She stood in front of the bag, growling. She didn't trust it anymore.

The phone would ring a few times a day, but almost no one I knew was calling. No one was allowed to call without a good reason. My mother wanted to keep the phone free for important news. My oma couldn't call us at all, neither could my uncles and aunts, nor my parents' friends.

'I don't want small talk,' my mother said. 'It just makes me nervous.'

When the phone rang it was usually someone from headquarters. The people at headquarters sent out doctors like my father. They knew exactly where the war was. They had chosen a place for my father. They had told him he was needed there, and he had packed his bag and taken off.

The people from headquarters always wanted to talk to my mother. They didn't say much to me. One time a lady phoned who called me sweetheart.

'Hello, sweetheart,' she said. 'Is your mother home?'

'Is it about my father?' I asked.

The lady who called me sweetheart hesitated a moment. Then she said, 'Why don't you let me talk to your mother. There's nothing the matter, dear.'

My mother grabbed the phone out of my hand. 'Hello?' she said.

I had never been to headquarters. I had no idea what it was like there. It must be a big building, because there are so many wars in the world. And floods and earthquakes too. And they need doctors everywhere. That kind of stuff can't fit into a small office.

There must even be a map on the wall with those little flags on pins that you can stick into it. For every doctor there must be a special little flag. My father's must be blue, because blue is his favourite colour. Or red, because he's got red hair. Maybe the lady who called me sweetheart was standing in front of the map holding the little flag in her hand. Because where could she put it if someone was missing?

I guess phone conversations weren't enough. My mother had to go to headquarters in person. She left in the morning in her car.

When I came home after school she wasn't back yet. I took the dog leash from the coat rack. I had promised to walk Mona. Mona climbed off the couch and walked over to me slowly. She could hardly believe that she would be allowed to go out with me. She knew I couldn't stand taking her for a walk.

It was warm outside. Mona tottered along behind me, panting. After a few minutes I had to stop for her to pee against a tree. When she was done we walked a little further. Until the next tree. When she wanted to sit down again I yanked on the leash. I was afraid she would poop, because I didn't have a bag with me.

A big black dog ran around a little field at the end of the street. Mona barked. The dog came over to us. He stood still in front of Mona and wagged his tail.

Mona doesn't like other dogs. She doesn't like

other people either. In fact she only likes my father and my mother. And she likes me a bit too, because she has to. The black dog seemed to like everyone. He looked at us and wagged his tail. He wanted to play.

Mona growled. I thought the dog would get mad. That he would bite Mona. That he would eat her up. Completely. He could gobble up such a weird fat little dog in one big bite. She shouldn't have been so uppity. But the black dog turned around and ran off across the field. Mona started barking at him. I pulled her away, back home.

Halfway down our street I met Margie. She was carrying a violin case on her back. 'Hi,' she said.

'Hi,' I said.

'It's so awful about your dad,' Margie said. 'That he's lost and everything.'

'How do you know that?' I asked.

'My mother told me,' said Margie. 'How horrible. I think your father is a hero.'

'A hero?'

'Yes. Because he goes off to help people. Even if it's dangerous.'

'Oh,' I said. 'Hero' was a weird word and it didn't fit my father at all. 'Hero' was something from a book or a movie. But in a book or a movie I wouldn't be out on the street with a dog like Mona. I'd be searching for my father and wouldn't be afraid of stray bullets.

Suddenly I saw my father as though he were standing right in front of me. I thought about that word 'hero' and because it didn't fit my father, I saw him just exactly the way he really was. I saw his red hair and his freckly face and his green eyes, green with little specks. My throat hurt. I couldn't swallow.

'Are you going to cry?' Margie asked.

'No,' I said.

'It's okay to cry,' Margie said.

'Mind your own business,' I said.

On the way home my mother had picked up my oma. The three of us sat around in the backyard.

My mother talked about headquarters. 'I didn't find out very much,' she said. 'Nobody knows exactly what is happening. But they are full of hope.'

'Good hope?' my oma asked.

'They say a lot of things could have gone wrong,' my mother said. 'With the transport, with the equipment. And they haven't had any information about...' She looked at me. 'Well, about anything serious. And now they are searching.'

'Margie thinks that Daddy is a hero,' I said.

My oma shook her head. My mother fidgeted with a little branch of the butterfly bush.

'Perhaps Margie is right,' my mother said. 'To some people Daddy is a hero.'

'Who?' I asked.

'The people who need him,' my mother said. 'The people who are wounded or sick. The people who would die without a doctor.'

'Oh no, no,' my oma said. 'Not a hero. To me he is not a hero. He's too self-centred to be a hero.'

'Let's not talk about that now,' my mother said.

'It's true,' my oma said. 'He thinks too much about himself and not enough about others. He's never at home. He's almost always on the go. And he's always seeking out danger.'

'It's not that bad,' my mother said.

'And he's always been that way,' my oma said. 'Always!'

She started to talk louder and louder. She's like a firecracker – all it takes to make her explode is a little flame. And you never know in advance whether you're that little flame.

'He was only a little kid,' my oma said. 'Five years old. He climbed on his tricycle and took off. I looked the other way for a second and he was gone. And I searched all over the place. I asked everywhere. I found him at the butcher. There he was, waiting for a slice of sausage. But the butcher shop was on the other side of the railroad tracks!'

'That has nothing to do with it,' my mother said. 'That has nothing to do with right now.'

'But he's always been that way!' my oma said. 'In the middle of the night he would go swimming. In the canal. And he rode a motorcycle into the Kalahari!'

'What's the Kalahari?' I asked.

'A desert,' my mother said.

'Did he go for a motorcycle ride in the desert?' I asked.

'Yes!' my oma said.

'None of this has anything to do with what's happening now,' my mother said.

'Of course it does,' said my oma. 'It has everything to do with it. He's only thinking of himself. He courts danger. He is in the middle of a war and we are worried about him.'

'He's a doctor,' my mother said. 'He goes there to help.'

'I know a lot of doctors,' my oma said. 'And they are staying right here.'

For a short while it was quiet.

'I'm going upstairs,' I said.

My father was so horribly lost. First because of what Margie had said and now because of what my oma said.

I stood up and went to my room. The windows were open. I could hear my mother and my oma talking, but I didn't listen to what they were saying.

I sat at my desk. I drew a picture of a dead dog. He was lying on his back with all four legs sticking straight up. Next to the dog I drew a man with a rifle. Bullets were coming out of the rifle. The dog was full of holes.

My mother knocked on the door.

'Yes?' I said.

The door opened a little. 'It's me,' my mother said.

'I know,' I said.

'Oma has gone home.'

'I know that too.'

'You know everything,' my mother said. She looked at my drawing. 'Are you angry?'

'Why?'

'You're making an angry drawing.'

I drew another hole in the dead dog. My mother had got it right. I was angry. But I was not quite sure at whom.

'Oma's right,' I said. 'Daddy is only thinking about himself.'

'Oma is saying that because she's worried.'

'But it's true.' I took a black pencil and scratched all over the dog. The paper tore.

'Whoa, whoa,' my mother said. She grabbed my hand. I kept holding on to the pencil.

'Don't do that,' my mother said.

Then I got really mad. I screamed. I yelled until my head was full of noise. I pushed my mother. I kicked my desk. The pencils flew all over the floor. My mother tried to grab me. 'Leave me alone!' I yelled. I kicked the little chest without legs. Squeaky's cage fell down. The top flew off.

'Watch it,' my mother said. 'Watch out for the mouse.'

I stopped screaming. The cage was lying on its side. It was cracked. Most of the sawdust had spilled. Squeaky was gone.

'Where is he?' I asked.

My mother kneeled down and looked around. 'Squeaky!' she called.

'Squeaky!' I called. I crawled on my knees around the room. My mother crawled behind me. We crawled through the sawdust.

I started to cry.

'Squeaky,' my mother said. 'Squeaky!' And all of a sudden she began to laugh.

'Squeaky, Squeaky,' I said, and I laughed too. I was laughing and crying. Not both at once. I took turns laughing and crying.

Squeaky was under my bed. I lay flat on my stomach and caught him. He didn't try to run away. When I grabbed him I could feel him trembling.

'Are you okay now?' my mother asked.

I nodded. We were sitting on the floor, leaning against my bed. Squeaky was sitting in my hand. He was trembling a little less.

'I just exploded,' I said. If my oma was a firecracker, then I was a cannonball. Of the two of us, I could make the loudest explosion. I had never known that before.

'It's nerves,' my mother said. She put her arm around me. 'It's going to be all right.'

I wanted to ask whether she was sure. But I was afraid she would say no. 'Is Oma right?' I asked.

'Don't pay attention to Oma. She always exaggerates.'

'But is she right?'

'Yes and no,' my mother said. 'You really need to understand one thing, Kiki. It's not so simple. Nobody is just good or just bad. Nobody thinks only about other people. Everyone thinks about themselves too. Even Daddy.'

'Then he isn't a hero,' I said.

'Fortunately not,' my mother said. 'I wouldn't want to think that. Give me a normal human being anytime.'

I picked up Squeaky's cage. It was really cracked.

'You'll need a new cage,' my mother said. 'You should go to the pet store tomorrow.'

'Would you?' I asked.

We started working on my mother's new project – the buffet. Someone from the store delivered it in a van. The buffet was big, but you could take it apart. Soon the living room was full up with its separate pieces – cabinets we would have to stack on top of each other later to make it into one huge buffet. But first my mother wanted to paint everything yellow. And before she could start painting, the old paint had to be scraped off. I helped her.

It was a lot of work. Some cabinets had ridges and rims, and there were also drawers with wooden knobs. It was going to be ugly. I could see that right away. My mother had bought a can of bright yellow paint. I didn't like it. But it was fun to scrape and not think about anything else. The radio was on. Once in a while we sang along with it.

We scraped the whole afternoon until my mother said, 'That's enough for today. I still have some errands to do.'

'Are you going to the pet store?' I asked.

'No,' she answered. 'You can do that yourself.'

'I hate the pet store.'

'It's your mouse.'

'Please!' I said. 'Just this time?'

'Okay. Just this time.' My mother took a shopping bag and went outside. But she stuck her head through the kitchen window. 'What's wrong with the pet store exactly?'

'Nothing,' I said. 'It's just such a stupid store.'

The news was on the radio. I heard my father's name.

'Mum!' I called.

My mother stuck her head in the kitchen window as far as she could.

The newsperson spoke very calmly. He was not talking to my mother and me, but to everyone. He said that my father had been missing for some time. He said, 'There is concern for his safety. The search action already underway has not produced any results.' After that he read the weather forecast.

My mother pulled her head back out. She walked through the yard to the front door and came in. 'Are you all right?' she asked. 'Did you get a scare?'

'Is something going on?' I asked. 'Something bad for Daddy?'

'No. There's nothing new going on. But Daddy has been missing for more than a week, and this is what happens.'

She turned the radio off. 'It's better not to listen.' The shopping bag fell on the floor. 'Shall I stay home? With you? I can go shopping tomorrow.'

I didn't want her to stay home. I was afraid that the next day I would have to buy a new mouse cage myself. 'Really, I can stay home on my own,' I said.

I kept on scraping the buffet by myself. I scraped a little ridge. And then the front side of a drawer. My mother had been gone for quite a while. I turned the radio on again. There was only music. I pushed all the buttons until I found a news station. It had already started. The newsperson was saying, 'There is concern for his safety.'

Now that I was all by myself, it sounded much worse. The words were kind of hanging in the air. I couldn't tell what they meant. It was like every-thing had to get into my brain through a tiny hole in my head. But after a while I did understand – the news was about being afraid. They were afraid some-thing was wrong. And if they were afraid, something must be wrong.

I waited for something to happen. Something inside me. But nothing happened. I didn't get scared. I didn't get angry. I felt nothing. And that nothing felt worse than a swarm of stray bullets. I grabbed Mona's leash from the coat rack and said, 'We're going out.'

Mona had a hard time keeping up with me. Past the field I took a right and then a left. I zigzag-ged through our neighbourhood. After a while we reached a little bridge that went over the expressway. Mona panted. She could barely keep up. We were standing near the concrete stairs of the pedestrian overpass.

'Come on,' I said.

Mona sat down. She wheezed.

'Come on,' I repeated. I pulled at the leash, but Mona didn't move. I bent down and lifted her up. I held her tight against me. Her front paws were on my shoulder. I held her behind with my hands. She panted in my ear. Sometimes she stopped panting in order to swallow, but then she'd start up again.

I walked up the stairs. It was a little bit breezy at the top of the overpass. Underneath cars hummed by. I walked to the railing and leaned over. Mona's paws scratched at my shoulder.

'Come on,' I said again, and I grabbed her collar. I stretched out my arms and lifted her over the railing.

A truck rumbled under the bridge.

I stood still, holding my arms out over the railing. Mona felt heavier and heavier. I could barely hold on to her anymore. Any moment now I would drop her. I didn't have to do anything. I just had to let go. That was all.

Mona stayed frozen. She didn't even wiggle.

I heard someone yell, 'Hey, you!'

This was the moment to drop Mona. 'Don't do it, don't do it, don't do it,' I said to myself.

But I did it anyway. I let go of Mona with one hand. She was hanging over the highway by her collar. Her leash was hanging down too.

'Watch out!' said a voice. Arms came around me. They were long arms. They reached around Mona too, and grabbed her tight.

Someone turned me around, away from the railing, and carefully lifted Mona out of my arms. It was my father. I could feel that it was my father. I had made the odds smaller. I had made the odds so small that nothing could happen anymore. He had come home. I looked up at his face.

It was not him. It was just a man. He had black hair and brown eyes, and he looked at me angrily. 'What the hell do you think you're doing?'

I couldn't answer.

The man put his hand on my shoulder. With his other hand he held Mona's leash. 'Calm down,' he said.

Was he talking to me or to Mona? I wanted to run away. He wasn't my father. He was taller and skinnier and he was wearing a striped shirt.

'I need to go home,' I said.

'I'll take you home,' the man said.

'Get lost,' I said.

'That's enough,' the man said. 'Are you totally nuts? Dropping a dog on the highway! Listen carefully, little girl. I'm taking you home or I'm taking you to the police. You tell me!' He grabbed my T-shirt hard.

———————

He should have been my father. He should have been my father, but he wasn't. And now he had grabbed me and was talking to me. He pushed me toward the stairs. 'Where do you live?' he asked.

It was a very ordinary question and maybe that was what made it happen. Suddenly I felt that everything that had just taken place was really weird. Suddenly I felt just like my regular, ordinary plain self again. And I had almost done something really bad.

On the top step of the stairs my knees kind of folded. I sat down.

'What's up with you now?' the man said.

'I didn't really want to do it,' I said. 'Not really. I held on to her, didn't I?'

The man sat down next to me. 'You gave me an awful scare,' he said. 'I can't stand people who hurt animals. I can't stand it.'

'I didn't know what I was doing.'

The man looked at me. 'Does that happen to you often?'

'No,' I said. But then I remembered the mouse and the pet store. I had done some pretty strange things lately. 'I don't know,' I said.

'What do you mean, you don't know?'

And then I told him everything. I told him about my father and about making the odds smaller. I told him everything except my dream about stray bullets because I had already told my mother about it and that was enough.

'Well,' said the man. 'That's quite a story.' He patted Mona. Mona growled, but he didn't pay attention. 'It's very serious,' he said. 'I can understand.'

He didn't say everything would work out, and I was glad. Because nobody could know if everything would work out.

'But what you said about those odds isn't quite right,' the man said. 'It doesn't work that way. I don't believe that you can make odds larger or smaller. Not like this.' He looked at me. 'Can I ask you something?'

I didn't answer. I thought he wanted to ask me something important, but I wasn't quite sure I wanted him to.

'What would your father think about all this?' the man asked.

The answer popped into my head right away. The whole time it had just been waiting around a little corner. Now that someone had asked the right question, it jumped out.

My father would never drop Mona. He would never think up the stuff about dead mice and dead dogs. Not even if I was missing. Not even if my mother and I were both missing.

'I want to go home,' I said to the man.

'You want me to come along?' he asked.

I shook my head.

'I wanted to talk to your parents about what happened,' the man said. 'Well, to your mother anyway. But maybe I don't need to now.'

'No,' I said.

He handed over Mona's leash. 'You'll never do it again?'

'No. Never.' I picked up Mona and carried her down the stairs.

'Hey,' called the man.

I turned around.

'Hang in there!' he called.

I had no idea what that meant. But it sounded like something solid and safe. 'You too,' I called back.

He raised his hand and waved.

I walked home slowly. Mona toddled along behind me. She wasn't even mad at me. She had no idea what was going on, I thought. I had almost dropped her and it didn't bother her at all. But it bothered me. Everything bothered me. My legs. They were weak and shaky. My arms. They were sore from hanging her over the railing. And my head especially. It was so full of horrible thoughts that it hurt.

What if that man hadn't been there? What would have happened? That was the most horrible thought. What would my mother do if she found out? And what would my father do? Those were the second-worst thoughts.

I didn't know if I really would have dropped Mona. Maybe I would have. Maybe not. I thought about how it would have been if I had. How she would have fallen down between the cars. I didn't want to think about it, but I couldn't help it. My head kept thinking on its own. I thought of the squished cats and squirrels that I sometimes saw lying along the road. Mona would have looked like that, but with more blood. My stomach began to feel queasy. I just kept thinking about blood. I felt like I was going to be sick. It was kind of a punishment. Punishment for something I hadn't done, but I'd almost done. Almost done for real.

And something else was really bothering me. Something I really couldn't stand to think about. But now I had to face it. The man said you can't make odds larger or smaller. Not the way I had thought I could. And I knew he was right.

My mother was waiting for us at the corner of our street. 'Where were you?' she said. 'I was worried. I can't handle any more trouble, Kiki.'

'I don't feel well,' I said. 'I want to go to bed.'

She put her arm around me. 'You look awful,' she said. 'What's the matter?'

'I don't know,' I said.

'How are you doing?' my mother asked. She was sitting on the edge of my bed.

'Not too bad,' I said.

She put her cheek against my forehead. 'You don't have a fever,' she said. 'You're not hot.'

'I'm cold. And I have a headache.'

'A mild stomach flu,' my mother said. 'Kiki?'

'Yes.'

'I need to talk to you. I went to the pet store to get a new cage for Squeaky.'

I turned over and lay with my face to the wall.

'Are you listening?' my mother asked. 'The boy in the pet store told me something. Something about you. It was kind of a strange story.'

'Mice,' I said. 'Mice and dogs.'

'Yes,' my mother said. 'Mice and dogs. What's going on, Kiki? Explain it to me.'

I explained it to her. I didn't say anything about the overpass, but I told her about making odds smaller and about the mouse that I had buried in the yard.

'But why did you do all of this so secretly?' she asked.

I turned around and looked at her.

'Because,' I said.

'That isn't an answer.'

'You would have been mad at me.'

'I wouldn't. But I would have told you it was a dumb thing to do. Do you really think that dead mice can change things?'

'It was only one dead mouse,' I said.

'And a dead little dog.'

'There wasn't a dead little dog.'

'Fortunately not,' she said. 'But you need to understand...'

'I do understand,' I said.

'But why did you do it, then?'

'Because at first I didn't understand.'

'Move over a bit.' My mother crawled into bed

next to me and took me in her arms. She smelled like fried potatoes and garlic.

'I hoped that Mona would die,' I said.

'That's not so very bad.'

'That is very bad,' I said.

My mother hugged me tightly. 'Keeks,' she said. 'You are worried. And when you're worried, you think strange thoughts.'

'You too?' I asked.

She gave a soft laugh. 'Me too. I think about Daddy's underwear, for instance. I'm sure he has run out of clean underwear. And clean socks. I never normally think about clean socks or underwear, but suddenly I'm thinking about them every day.'

'I thought about little dogs all the time,' I said. 'I wanted to kill one.'

'No,' my mother said. 'Not really.'

'How do you know?'

'I just know. Thinking and doing, those are two different things. If you only knew all the things I've been thinking about. All the people I have murdered in my thoughts.'

'Tell me who?' I asked.

'That's a secret.'

'Oma,' I said.

My mother didn't answer.

'Me,' I said.

'No,' my mother said. 'Not you. Never you.'

I was getting hot under the covers. 'Why don't you get up?' I said.

'You want to get up too?' my mother asked. 'Or are you still sick?'

'I don't want to go to school tomorrow,' I said. 'Everybody knows about Daddy now.'

It was strange just staying home. Outside all sorts of things were going on. The garbage truck went past, the mail came through the mail slot, and a lady with a baby in a stroller walked by on the footpath. Everything outside was happening as usual. My mother had to take Mona to the vet. It was time for her shots.

Margie came over that afternoon. 'Are you doing a bit better?' she asked.

I shrugged.

'I made a drawing for you.' Margie held up a sheet of paper. 'Can you see what it is?'

'A face,' I said.

'Your father,' Margie said.

The top half of the drawing was orange pencil scratches.

'But what's that?' I asked.

'His hair,' Margie said.

There was a word at the bottom of the drawing. It was written in large black letters: MISSING.

'I'm not so good at painting,' Margie said. 'It always turns out messy. That's why I did it in pencil. It's a poster. To put up. Because your father is missing and because I hope they'll find him soon.'

'Thank you very much,' I said.

'Are you going to tape it up in the window?'

'Later.'

'I can't stay,' Margie said. 'I have to go home. Tomorrow I need to perform Vivaldi with vibrato.'

'Is that something you do in gymnastics?' I asked.

Margie looked at me. 'No. Of course not. You do vibrato with a violin.'

My mother laughed when she saw the poster.

'Where are you going to put it?' she asked.

'I'm not going to put it anywhere,' I answered.

'Margie won't like that.' She held up the sheet of paper. 'Up at the top, is that his hair?'

'Yes.'

'I can't believe it.'

I looked at the face in the drawing. Below the orange scratches Margie had drawn two round eyes with thin pencil lines. The nose was a firm straight line and the mouth was slightly open. You could see a row of teeth.

'Let's be nice to Margie,' my mother said. She put the drawing on the table and got a roll of tape from the kitchen drawer.

I didn't want to be nice to Margie. Somewhere, very far away, my father was missing. It was ridiculous to put up a poster here, on our street.

'Well?' my mother said.

'No,' I said. 'I don't want to put it up.'

'Come on now,' my mother said.

'No!' I said. 'Next thing everyone will think that I made it.'

'Margie means well. Maybe this is just her way.'

'Her way?'

'Her way to help.'

'It's a scary drawing,' I said.

'We'll put it up somewhere in a corner, out of the way,' my mother said.

'She wants us to tape it to the window. So everyone can see it.'

'So, let's do it,' my mother said. 'I'll tape it to your window and you go out to the yard to see whether it's straight.'

I went out to the yard and looked up. After a while my mother appeared behind the window of my room. She taped the drawing to the windowpane, all the way down in the corner. You couldn't really read the writing. I could only see the top part. I couldn't really make out what the picture was about. Something orange, that was all. Margie's pencil lines were too thin.

'It's okay!' I yelled.

I liked having the buffet around. Occasionally I scraped it a little. When my mother was home, she helped me.

I didn't want to think about dead dogs. I didn't want to think about my father either. That was hard because there wasn't much else to think about. Nothing was really happening. I told myself my mother was right—thinking and doing were two different things. But still I tried to think as little as possible. Just to be sure.

Sometimes Mona would come and sit next to me. Ever since I hung her over the highway, she liked me a lot better. Maybe she was a little more fond of me because I hadn't let go of her. Or perhaps she thought it was exciting. Maybe she thought the overpass was a kind of amusement-park ride for dogs. Whee!

Mona knew I wasn't a dog murderer. My mother knew I wasn't a dog murderer. They had to be right. I didn't let go of Mona in the end.

I scraped and scraped the buffet and after two days I had finished.

My mother and I each had a brush. My mother pried open the paint can with a screwdriver. She stirred the yellow paint with a piece of wood.

'Pay close attention.' She dipped her brush in the paint and wiped it against the rim of the can. She painted part of a cabinet door. 'About this thick. And watch out that it doesn't drip.'

I dipped my brush in the paint. Some paint got on the handle. When I squeezed the brush against the rim of the can I got paint on my fingers.

'Pretty difficult, no?' my mother said.

'Not at all,' I said.

Each of us painted a cabinet door. My mother's was streaky. 'That's how it's supposed to be. It needs a second coat.'

My cabinet door looked drippy.

———

The telephone rang. My mother picked it up. 'Yes?' she said. Then for a long time she listened. Now and then she said, 'yes' or 'no' or 'hmmm'. Her face turned red. 'Where?' she asked.

'Who is it?' I asked. She put her finger to her lips.

'Okay,' she said into the phone. 'Okay, I'll wait for that.' She pushed the button down and kept holding the phone in her hand. 'That was headquarters,' she said.

I couldn't tell whether she was sad or happy. 'About Daddy?' I said.

She nodded.

'What did they say?' I asked.

'They might have found him,' my mother answered. 'They're not sure, Kiki. They said maybe.'

I got hot. My whole body started to tingle.

'How's that possible?' I said. 'Maybe!'

My mother gave a couple of deep sighs. 'I need to stay calm,' she said. 'Can you understand that?'

'Yes.'

'They heard that someone was found. Behind the front lines. It could be Daddy. It almost has to be Daddy.'

'It is Daddy,' I said.

She shook her head quickly. 'They aren't sure. We won't say anything yet. To anyone. Not even Oma.'

'What does that mean – behind the front lines?' I asked.

For a moment she stared at her cabinet door. 'That means behind where the soldiers are fighting.'

'That's good,' I said. 'Right?'

'Yes,' my mother said. But she did not sound very sure.

I wanted to be happy. I wanted to put up decorations and bake a cake and dance around in the living room. But it wasn't possible yet. It was almost possible. They had almost found my father. He would almost come home. I nearly blew up because of all the things that were almost happening.

My mother stayed right by the phone. There were so many calls and each time she picked it up she was so nervous. When she talked I watched her face, but I could see that she wasn't getting important news. She never started laughing or crying. She just kept getting more and more nervous.

I painted all day because I wanted to have something to do. My mother didn't really help. She kept doing one thing after another. She would walk around the room, sit on the couch and immediately get up again. She didn't do any errands. At the end of the day she ordered pizza on the phone. A boy on a scooter delivered two pizzas. We ate them out of the boxes on our laps. But we weren't very hungry. We had lots of leftovers.

Mona had to go outside. I went with her and waited while she peed and pooped. When she was done I lifted her up and ran home.

'Why don't you go to sleep?' my mother said around eleven o'clock.

'No,' I said. 'I'm going to wait.'

'Time goes faster when you're sleeping,' she said.

I walked upstairs to my room. Squeaky was sitting in his night cage. His water bottle was empty and he had nothing to eat. I filled the bottle in the bathroom. And then I threw a handful of mouse food into the cage. I got my blanket and took it downstairs with me.

'I'm going to sleep on the couch,' I said to my mother.

'No, no,' she said. 'The paint has fumes.'

'So what?'

'You'll get a headache.'

'So what?'

We looked at each other. My mother shrugged. 'Go ahead, then,' she said.

I lay on the couch under the blanket. My mother sat at the other end. I put my feet on her lap. Mona jumped up on a chair. She turned around a few times and plopped down. After a while she began to snore.

I tried my very best not to think about anything. But the more I tried, the less my brain wanted to obey. I heard Mona snore and I thought about the overpass. I had not dropped Mona, and now I was a girl without a dead dog. There was a dead mouse buried in the yard, but I did not have a dead dog. Maybe a dead mouse wasn't enough. Maybe they wouldn't find my father after all. Maybe it wasn't my father behind the front lines. Maybe it was someone else.

'You're tossing and turning,' my mother said.

'I can't sleep. I keep thinking about Daddy all the time.'

'Try to count sheep. Say one-sheep-two-sheep, three-sheep-four-sheep,' my mother said.

———

'Don't be silly,' I said.

'Oma does that all the time,' my mother said. 'She herself told me that. Whenever she's worried she repeats over and over, one-sheep-two-sheep, three-sheep-four-sheep. And then she has no trouble falling asleep.'

I said, 'One-sheep-two-sheep, three-sheep-four-sheep, one-sheep-two-sheep, three-sheep-four-sheep.'

'You need to say it softly,' my mother said. 'And slowly.'

Very slowly I said, 'One-sheep-two-sheep, three-sheep-four-sheep.' As long as I was saying it, I couldn't think clearly. I should have known that earlier. I repeated it over and over, softer and softer, slower and slower.

My mother woke me up. Her cheeks were wet. She was crying. 'They found him,' she said.

I put my arms around her neck. I hugged her tight. 'When is he coming home?'

Her mouth was close to my ear. 'Soon,' she said. 'Very, very soon.'

'He has to come now,' I said.

She cried even harder. I could feel tears coming into my own eyes. It was easy to cry. The tears poured out.

'I'm crying because I'm happy,' I said. 'Isn't that weird?'

My mother almost smothered me. 'No, no,' she said.

'How about you?' I asked.

Slowly she let go of me. She wiped the tears off her cheeks. 'Yes,' she said. 'Of course I'm happy.'

I noticed that there was something else. Something she didn't want to say. I could see it on her face. She was staring blankly over my head, like she always does when she's trying to hide something from me.

'What is it?' I said.

'Daddy has had an accident.'

I started to feel dizzy. 'He is dead,' I said.

'No, Kiki,' my mother said. 'No, that's not it. Luckily, no, it's not.'

I took a deep breath. 'What is it?'

'An accident. Daddy got hurt.'

'Is it serious?'

'Everything will be all right in the end,' she said.

The dizziness went down into my stomach. The room was turning around me. My mother didn't notice. She was somewhere else, thinking her own thoughts. She knew something and I didn't.

'I want to know,' I said.

She put her hands over her face and sat on the edge of the couch for a moment. After a while she pulled her hands away and looked me straight in the eyes. 'A mine exploded. Daddy's car drove over it. I have no idea why he was there or even when he was there. I don't know very much yet.'

'It is serious,' I said.

It took her a while to answer. 'Yes,' she said. 'It is serious. His leg was...hurt.'

'What do you mean "hurt"?'

'He's in a hospital now. Not far from where they found him. But they want to bring him home as fast as possible. So they can help him.'

'But it's only his leg,' I said. 'How can that be serious?'

'If your leg is hurt, you can get very sick.'

'What are they going to do to him?' I asked. But I didn't need an answer. I could figure it out for myself. In wars land mines often explode. And the people on top of them can die. Or they can get really badly hurt, and then they need a doctor like my father. Sometimes their leg gets blown up and then it has to be cut off, because otherwise they would die. Later they walk around on crutches and have a little stump instead of a leg. And now a mine had exploded under my father's car.

'His leg needs to be cut off,' I said.

My mother nodded. 'Maybe.'

I started to gag. The pizza came up. I threw up on my blanket.

The washing machine was running. My mother and I lay on the bed together. I was on my father's side.

'Kiki,' my mother said.

'Yes?'

'You shouldn't worry.'

'No.'

'Sometimes things like this happen. You couldn't have made it any different. So you should stop thinking about mice and all that. Promise?'

'Yes,' I said.

I knew my mother was trying to help, but it would have been better if she hadn't brought the whole thing up again. Now I couldn't stop thinking about mice and all the odds.

Margie had a plastic cow in her room – Clara the Wonder Cow. If you pushed a button, she started to moo. Then she would swing her head back and forth and a little lamp in her udder would go on and off. A weird little voice would come out of her stomach, 'Milk, yummy milk. Milk, yummy milk.'

The first time I heard it, it was funny, but after a while you couldn't help hating Clara. I was starting to feel more and more like Clara the Wonder Cow. I didn't have a little voice in my stomach. I had a little voice in my head. I thought about Mona and mice and dead dogs. The same thing over and over. I had a Clara the Wonder Cow button in my head and my mother had just pushed it.

'One-sheep-two-sheep, three-sheep-four-sheep,' I said softly. It helped a little. I said it a few times, but I wanted to say something else. 'A mine is buried in the ground,' I said. 'And it explodes if you step on it. Or when your car drives over it. I mean, a mine just lies there waiting and nobody knows it's there. It's kind of like a stray bullet, but it can't fly.'

'Shh,' my mother said. 'We're going to sleep.'

My father didn't come home right away. A lot of things had to be organised first. My mother was on the phone all day. We wanted to talk to my father so badly, but he was too sick. There was a doctor who called a few times. He explained everything to my mother. I couldn't hear what he said. My mother told me there wasn't much news. My father slept almost all day and he took medicine. And he himself didn't seem to know just what had happened. That was because of the painkillers, my mother said.

I painted the buffet all by myself. Pretty soon all the doors and drawers were drippy yellow.

Everyone knew now that my father had been

found. We got cards and tons of flowers. When all our vases were full my oma brought over her vases. She cried while she fixed the flowers.

'Don't cry,' my mother said.

'No,' my oma said. But she kept right on crying anyway.

'Now I have to cry too,' my mother said.

It seems like crying is catching. I began to cry too.

'That's because it's over,' my mother said. 'It's a delayed reaction.'

Four days after he was found, my father was sent home on a plane. The plane landed at the airport and my mother went there. I had to stay home.

'But I want to see Daddy,' I said.

'You can't,' my mother said. 'Really. Daddy will be transferred immediately from the plane onto the ambulance, and then I have to organise a lot of things. Tomorrow you can see him. Tomorrow I'll take you to the hospital.'

The next day I saw my father, but from a distance. I saw him through a window. I stood in a corridor of the hospital and they let me peek through the window. It looked to me like my father had lots more injuries than just his leg. He lay completely still in bed.

'He's asleep,' my mother said.

Bags with little tubes attached were hanging over his bed. I saw my father's face sticking out from his sheet. There were dark blotches on his forehead and he had a swollen eye.

My oma tapped on the glass.

'He can't hear you,' my mother said.

When we came home my mother sat on the couch. Right in the middle. My oma sat down on one side of her and I sat down on the other. Mona walked back and forth. She was looking for a place on the couch. But my oma and I were taking up all the room. Mona sighed and jumped on a chair.

'I've talked to the doctors,' my mother said. 'First they hoped they could save his leg. But now they think maybe it would be better to amputate it.'

'That means his leg has to come off,' my oma said to me. 'That's really terrible, sweetheart. But that's how it is.'

I was not shocked. I didn't even get sick. Maybe

I had got over the shock. Maybe I had got used to the idea. I just felt tired. Really tired.

My oma patted my mother's knee. Then she said, 'Everything will be all right. I know someone with one leg. A very nice man. And he can do almost anything because he has an artificial leg with "thinking" hinges. Something like that would be wonderful.'

My mother shook her head. 'We're not that far yet. First he has to heal and learn how to walk again, and that will take a long time.'

'But that kind of a leg comes in handy,' my oma said.

'We won't be ready for that for a long time,' my mother said. 'For the time being he's too sick.'

'But later,' my oma said. 'Later it will come in handy. I'll ask that man about his artificial leg.'

'No,' my mother said. 'Please don't.'

'Stop it!' I yelled. 'Both of you!'

They looked at me.

My mother thought I should go to bed early. She took me upstairs and tucked me in. Then she closed the door quietly behind her.

I was tired, but I couldn't fall asleep right away. I climbed out of bed and walked over to the window. I tried to tear off Margie's drawing. But the tape was really sticking. The corners tore off.

Squeaky raced through his cage. Once in a while he stopped to dig in the sawdust. For a second I thought of Mona and the dead mouse. But they disappeared from my mind again quickly. I didn't even have to say one-sheep-two-sheep. My thoughts went in a different direction. I thought about the map at headquarters. Were they pinning a red flag on the spot where the hospital is right now?

My father came back. He was really back. I could hardly keep such a real thought inside me. My father was everywhere—in my room, in the house. The whole world was full of my father.

The next day I woke up late. My oma was in the kitchen. She was making French toast.

'Where is Mummy?' I asked.

'She's at the hospital.'

'How's Daddy?'

'He had an operation this morning.'

'Did they cut off his leg?'

'Amputated,' she said. 'His leg was amputated.'

I noticed that she was mad. 'But wasn't that the plan?' I said. 'Now he can get better again.'

She put two slices of French toast on a plate and pushed the plate into my hands. 'Don't let it get cold,' she said.

I sat down at the table. I wasn't hungry. The French toast looked greasy.

'Why are you mad?' I asked. 'Yesterday you said everything would be okay.'

My oma banged the frying pan on the counter. 'Can I be mad for a change? All of a sudden I've got a child with one leg.' She walked out of the kitchen. She slammed the living-room door shut, and I heard her stomping up the stairs. First upstairs and then downstairs again. She opened the door. 'I'm sorry,' she said. 'But I'm boiling mad. I brought him into the world as a whole being.' Then she slammed the door shut and stomped upstairs again.

I stayed at the table. When my mother came home the French toast was cold.

That night the three of us went to the hospital. My oma wanted to sit in the back of the car.

'Are you nervous about seeing Daddy?' my mother asked.

Of course I was nervous. I had never seen anyone who didn't have a leg. 'A little bit,' I said.

'It doesn't look scary,' my mother said. 'It's not too bad.'

'Oma is mad,' I whispered.

My mother looked in the mirror. 'I can understand that,' she said. 'Oma still has to absorb it all.'

'And you?'

'Me too,' my mother said. 'And you?'

'Me too,' I said. 'And you?'

She didn't answer.

'And you?' I said again.

'Is this a little game?' my mother asked. 'Me too. And you?'

'Me too,' I said. 'And you?'

'Me too,' my mother said.

'Why don't you stop that,' my oma called from the back seat. 'That's enough.'

Before the door to my father's room could open, I had to put on hospital clothes. The nurse tried to explain to me why it was necessary, but I didn't listen. I just wanted to get ready as fast as possible. I wanted to be with my father so badly that I forgot to get upset. They gave me plastic gloves and a gown with long sleeves, and I had to put on a cap and a mask over my mouth. I was afraid my father wouldn't recognise me, because you could only see my eyes.

But when I went in he woke up and said right

away, 'Hey Kiki.' His voice sounded a bit hoarse and deep – the way it did when he was going to tell a scary story. But now it wasn't on purpose.

On the other side of the window I could see my mother and my oma putting on their hospital clothes. My mother was pushing her arms into the sleeves of a gown.

'Hey Dad,' I said.

He looked at me. His eye was a little less swollen. 'Sweetheart,' he said.

I looked at the spot where my father's legs ought to be. They had made a tent on his bed. I couldn't tell which leg was still there. I only saw a bulging blue blanket. Bags with blood and something that looked like water were hanging over the bed. They were attached to my father with a little tube. Other bags were hanging from the railing. There was a bag with blood and a bag with pee. I sat on a stool next to the bed, as far away as possible from the bags and as close as possible to my father's head.

'Is everything going to be okay?' I asked.

My father stretched out his hand. I put my hand on top of his. My father stroked my plastic glove with his thumb.

'Yes,' he said. 'We're okay.' His eyes closed a little.
'How are things at home?' he asked.

'We got a new buffet,' I said.

My mother decided that I should go back to school again.

'But they'll ask all kinds of questions,' I said.

'Just tell them once what happened,' my mother said. She called Miss Anneke to explain what was going on.

The next morning I went to school. We had to sit in a circle.

'You all know that Kiki's father was missing,' Miss Anneke said. 'And that he was found. And that he is hurt. We're all very sad about that. Of course we're glad that Kiki is back in school again. Perhaps she can tell us how her father is doing now.

That would be nice.' Miss Anneke looked at me. 'Go ahead, Kiki.'

I told them that my father was in the hospital and that there had been an accident with a mine and that he was missing a leg now. Afterwards anyone could ask questions. But almost no one could think of a good question.

'Can't your father walk anymore?' Margie asked.

'Of course not,' I said. 'He just lost his leg. But later he'll get an artificial leg with "smart" hinges.'

'How does that work?' asked Joris.

'I don't know,' I said.

For a short while everyone was quiet. Then Farah said, 'That's really terrible for you.'

'Yes,' Margie said.

'Yes,' Joris said. 'Really terrible.'

After the circle talk Miss Anneke put her hand on my shoulder. 'Well done,' she said.

All the children and teachers tried really hard to be nice to me. It wasn't so great getting so much attention. I wanted everything to be normal again. The nicer everyone acted, the worse everything seemed. At three o'clock I was glad to go home.

If I was lucky my oma would be there. Maybe she would be grumpy. That would be great. Just what I needed.

But when I got home nobody was there. There was a note from my mother on the table:

Hi sweetheart,
Did it go all right today?
I'll be home at four o'clock.
Can you walk Mona?
Kiss,
Mummy

I took Mona outside. We walked to the field at the end of the street. The big black dog was there too. He came running over to Mona. Mona growled, but the black dog didn't pay attention. He stood in front of Mona wagging his tail and trying to sniff her nose.

'Go away,' I said to the dog.

He wagged his tail even more happily.

Suddenly Mona had had enough. She jumped up and bit the big black dog right on the nose. Pretty hard too, because he ran away yelping.

When we headed for home I was feeling much better. Mona too. She tottered behind me and sighed an awful stinky sigh. So awful the whole street could smell it.

My father was put in another room. We didn't need to wear hospital gowns anymore. The tent under the blanket had disappeared. And the best was that no more bags were hanging on the bed railing. The new room was big and crowded. There were eight beds and somebody was lying in each one.

So many people wanted to visit my father, but no more than two visitors at a time were allowed. So my mother made a list. We got to visit him the most.

My father slept most of the time. Lots of times when you were talking to him he closed his eyes. His face had got thin and there were circles under his eyes. No matter how much he slept, he still looked tired.

My mother said that was part of the process. 'You'll see,' she said. 'He will gradually get better.'

One afternoon I was sitting next to my father's bed. My mother was picking up my oma. I looked at the blanket. On the side where there was no leg, the bed looked empty and flat.

'Do you want to see it?' my father said.

'Yes,' I said.

He lifted the blanket and showed me his leg. It ended a little way below his knee. It was weird. A short little leg with no foot. I didn't feel upset. It was wrapped in a white bandage.

'Does it hurt?' I asked.

'Yes,' my father said. 'Sometimes it really hurts.'

'Mummy kept thinking of socks and underwear.'

He looked at me.

'When you were gone.'

'Really?' my father said. He pulled the blanket back up again.

'Yes,' I said. 'But now you won't need as many socks.'

He smiled for a second. 'That's good, then.'

'What's going to happen next?' I asked.

'Well,' my father said.

'You won't be able to travel anymore.'

My father sighed. 'Do you know the story of the man who was afraid of everything?'

'That's a stupid story.'

'Yes,' my father said. 'It is a stupid story. But I still don't want to become a man who is afraid of everything.'

'You only have *one* leg.'

'I know that,' my father said.

'You can't travel with just *one* leg.'

'Of course I can. Soon I'll get an artificial leg or a wheelchair, and then I can travel all over the world.'

'I don't want you to,' I said.

My father grabbed my hand. 'I'll just take you with me. You can push my wheelchair and polish my new leg and tell me all the time to be careful, and if it's dangerous, we'll keep a safe distance.' He pulled my hand up to his face. I could feel his scratchy cheek.

'At night I worry sometimes,' he said. 'Because I don't know how things will be from now on. I only know it will never be the same again. And that I won't ever be able to do things the same way.'

'If you are worried,' I said, 'you should say

---

one-sheep-two-sheep, three-sheep-four-sheep.'

'Does that work?'

'It works for me.'

'One-sheep-two-sheep, three-sheep-four-sheep.'

'Not so fast,' I said. 'And it should be softer.'

'One-sheep-two-sheep, three-sheep-four-sheep,' my father said softly.

I could hear my oma out in the hall. 'The tangerines were on sale. And I couldn't think of what else to bring. He likes tangerines, doesn't he?'

I could hear my mother too. 'Only the seedless ones,' she said.

'Let's pretend we're asleep,' I whispered.

My father closed his eyes. I bent over and put my head on his chest.

My oma and my mother came in. I squeezed my eyes shut.

'Are they asleep?' my oma asked.

'I think so,' my mother said.

I wanted to call out, 'Fooled you!' But I waited a moment. I could feel my father breathing. His chest was going up and down slowly.

MARJOLIJN HOF, formerly a children's librarian, always dreamed of being a writer. When *Against the Odds* (*Een kleine kans*), her first novel, was published it was met with high critical acclaim, winning three major Dutch and Flemish children's book prizes – the Golden Owl Juvenile Literature Prize, the Golden Owl Young Reader's Prize and the Golden Slate Pencil – and it has been translated into twelve languages. Marjolijn lives in Krommenie, the Netherlands.